To Lekky, Elly and Max

SIMON & SCHUSTER BOOKS FOR YOUNG READERS
Simon & Schuster Building, Rockefeller Center
1230 Avenue of the Americas, New York, New York 10020
Text copyright © 1991 by Jakki Wood.
Illustrations copyright © 1991 by Rog Bonner.

First U.S. edition 1992

Originally published in Great Britain
by ABC as *DADS ARE GREAT FUN*.
SIMON & SCHUSTER BOOKS FOR YOUNG READERS
is a trademark of Simon & Schuster.
Manufactured in Hong Kong

10 9 8 7 6 5 4 3 2 1

Library of Congress Cataloging-in-Publication Data
Wood, Jakki.
    Dads are such fun / by Jakki Wood ;
  illustrations by Rog Bonner.   p.   cm.   Summary: Animal and
human children declare why their dads are such fun.
    [1. Father and child—Fiction.   2. Animals—Fiction.]
I. Bonner, Rog, ill.   II. Title.   PZ7.W8495Dad
1992 [E]—dc20 91-21517 CIP ISBN: 0-671-75342-8

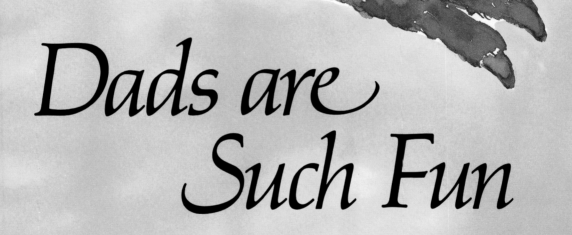

Dads are Such Fun

Words by Jakki Wood · Pictures by Rog Bonner

SIMON & SCHUSTER BOOKS FOR YOUNG READERS
Published by Simon & Schuster
New York · London · Toronto · Sydney · Tokyo · Singapore

My dad's
such fun.
He has
strong arms...

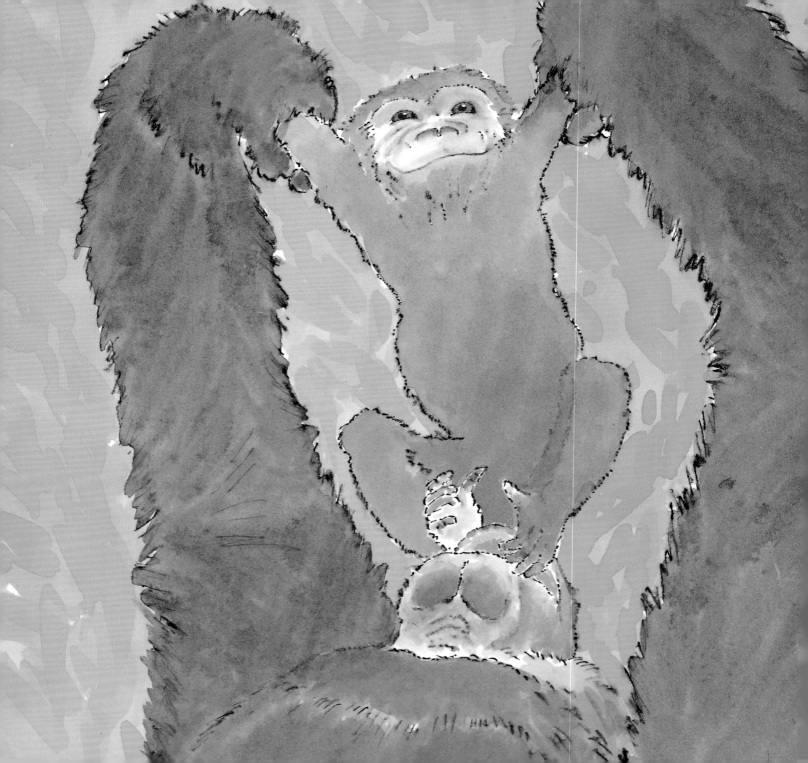

...to swing me
high in the air.

My dad's such fun.
We play all day...

...and then I get a
piggyback ride home.

My dad's got a
big long nose...

...which makes bathtime lots of fun.

My dad's such fun.
He's full of surprises.

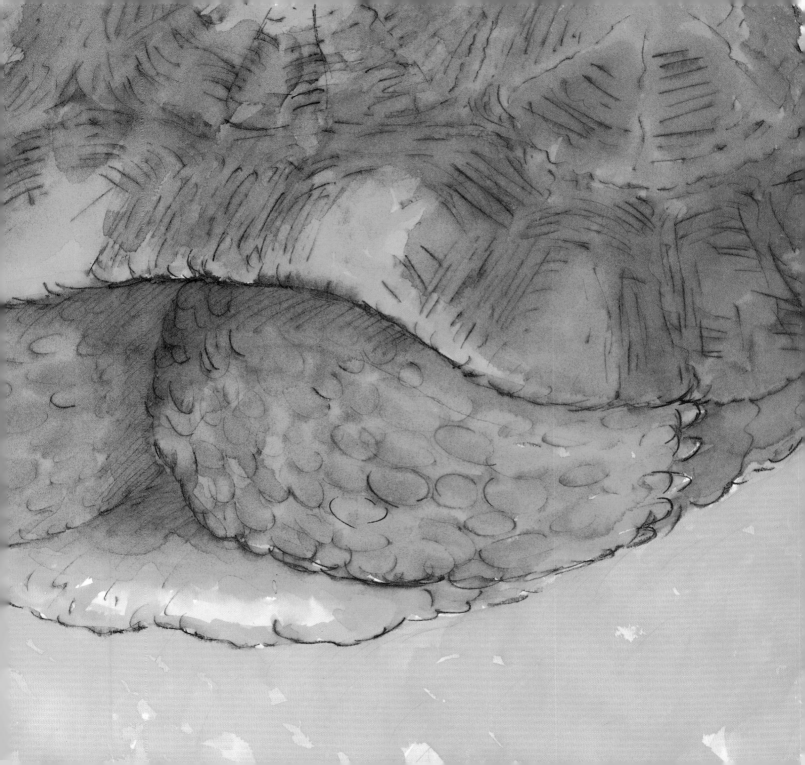

Peek-a-boo!

My dad roars at me sometimes...

...but he nuzzles and
kisses me, too.

Our dad has strong arms.
He gives us piggyback rides,
and makes bathtime fun.
He's full of surprises.
He roars at us sometimes...

...but he hugs and
kisses us, too.

Dads are such fun!